TABLE OF CONTENTS

D0002097

ALIENS

ALBERT

MR. TWIDDLE

MRS. TWIDDLE

CHAPTER ONE

Albert Twiddle lived in a house that looked like a palace.

It had a swimming pool.

It had a tennis court.

It even had its very own roller coaster.

YAAAAAAA!

Now that's what I call fun!

Albert's room was on the top floor. It was huge and full of amazing gadgets.

There was a sound system that was so loud it could shatter windows.

There were hundreds of video games.

And there was a TV the size of a movie screen.

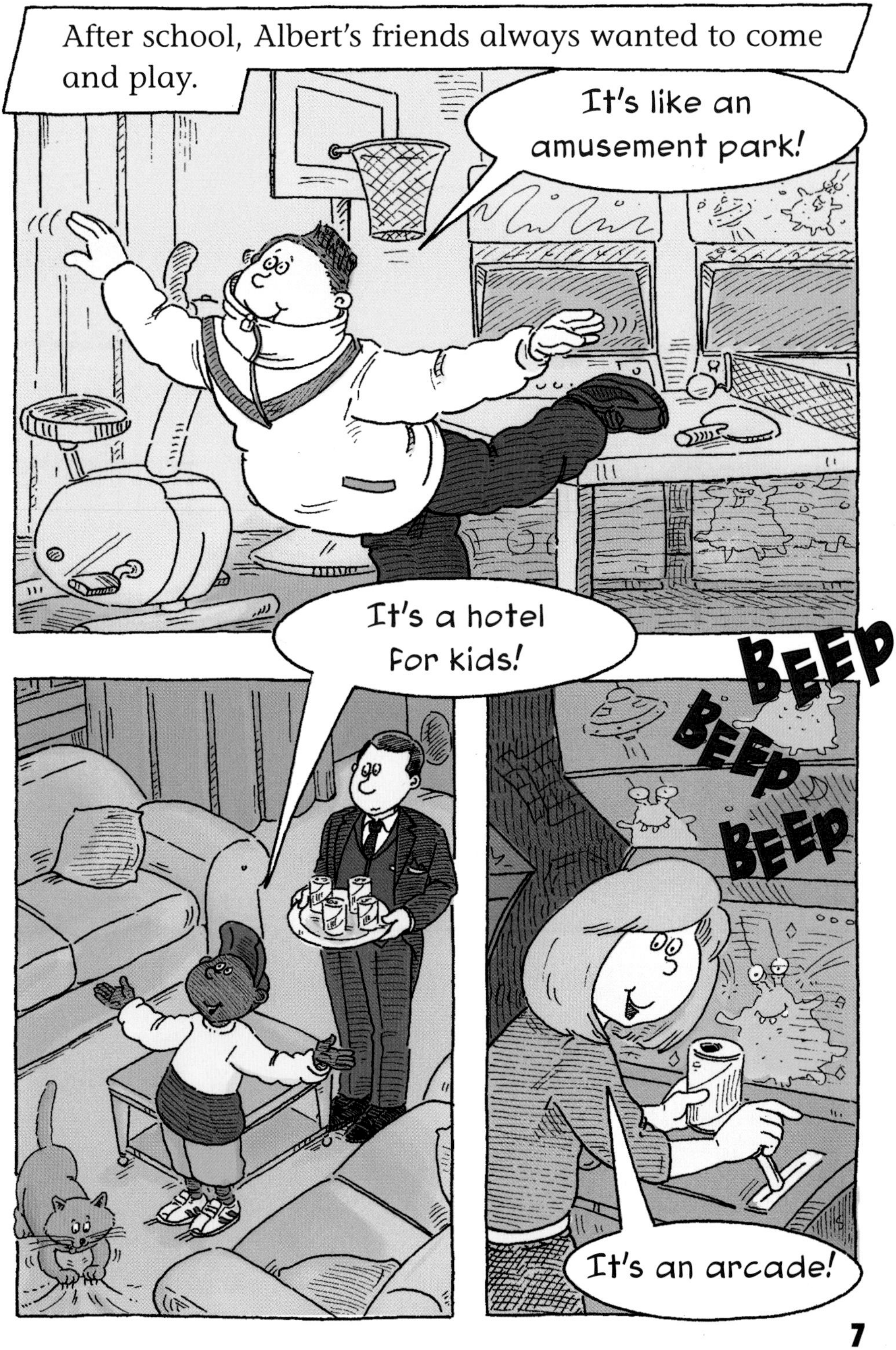
After school, Albert's friends always wanted to come and play.
It's like an amusement park!
It's a hotel for kids!
BEEP
BEEP
BEEP
It's an arcade!

As for the clothes that hung in Albert's closet . . .

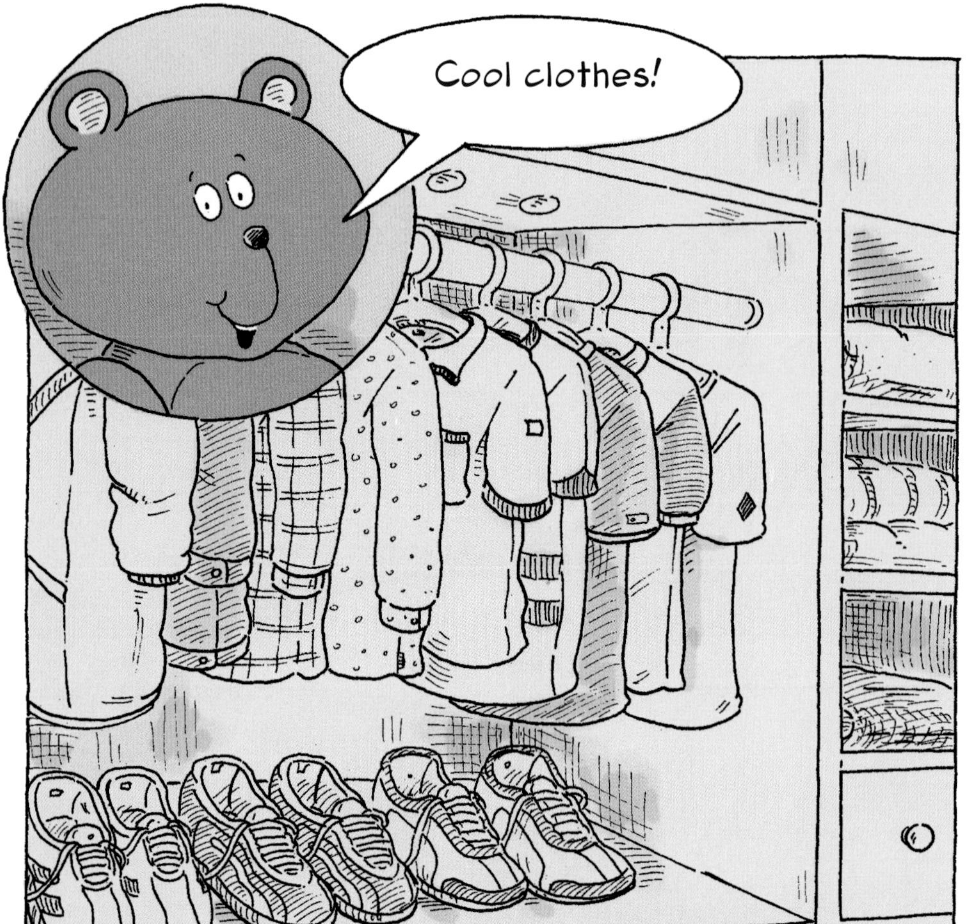
Cool clothes!

Albert had the coolest shoes, the coolest jeans, and the most expensive jackets you've ever seen.

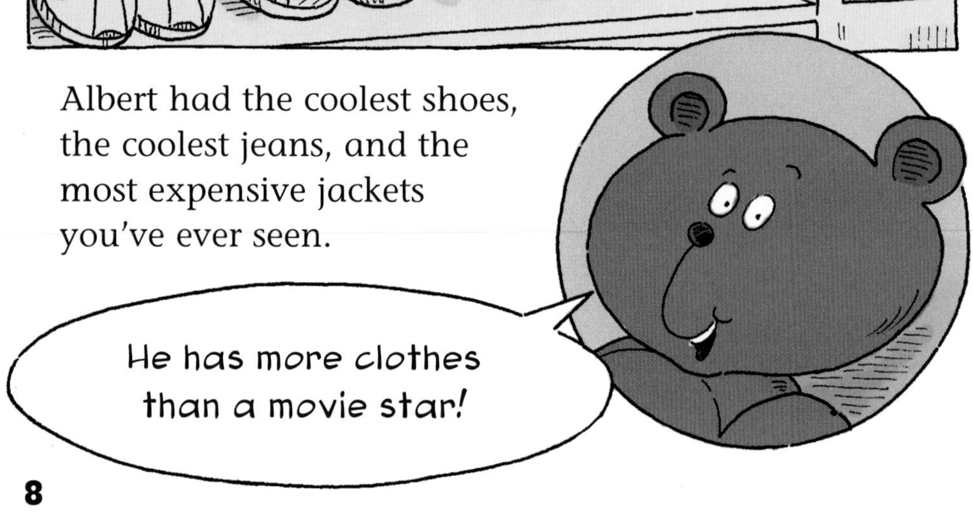
He has more clothes
than a movie star!

So why did Albert have so many fantastic things?

Because Mr. and Mrs. Twiddle were really, really successful. That's why!

Besides, with a name like Twiddle, you've got to have something going for you!

While other kids' dads drove used cars, Albert's father flew around the world in his very own jet.

When other kids walked home from school, Albert
rode home in a chauffeur-driven limousine.

Of course, Albert's friends thought his parents were really cool.

Their dads never went to New York on business trips. They stayed at home and watched TV.

Their moms never went away to fancy hotels. They cooked supper, and sometimes they made costumes for the school play.

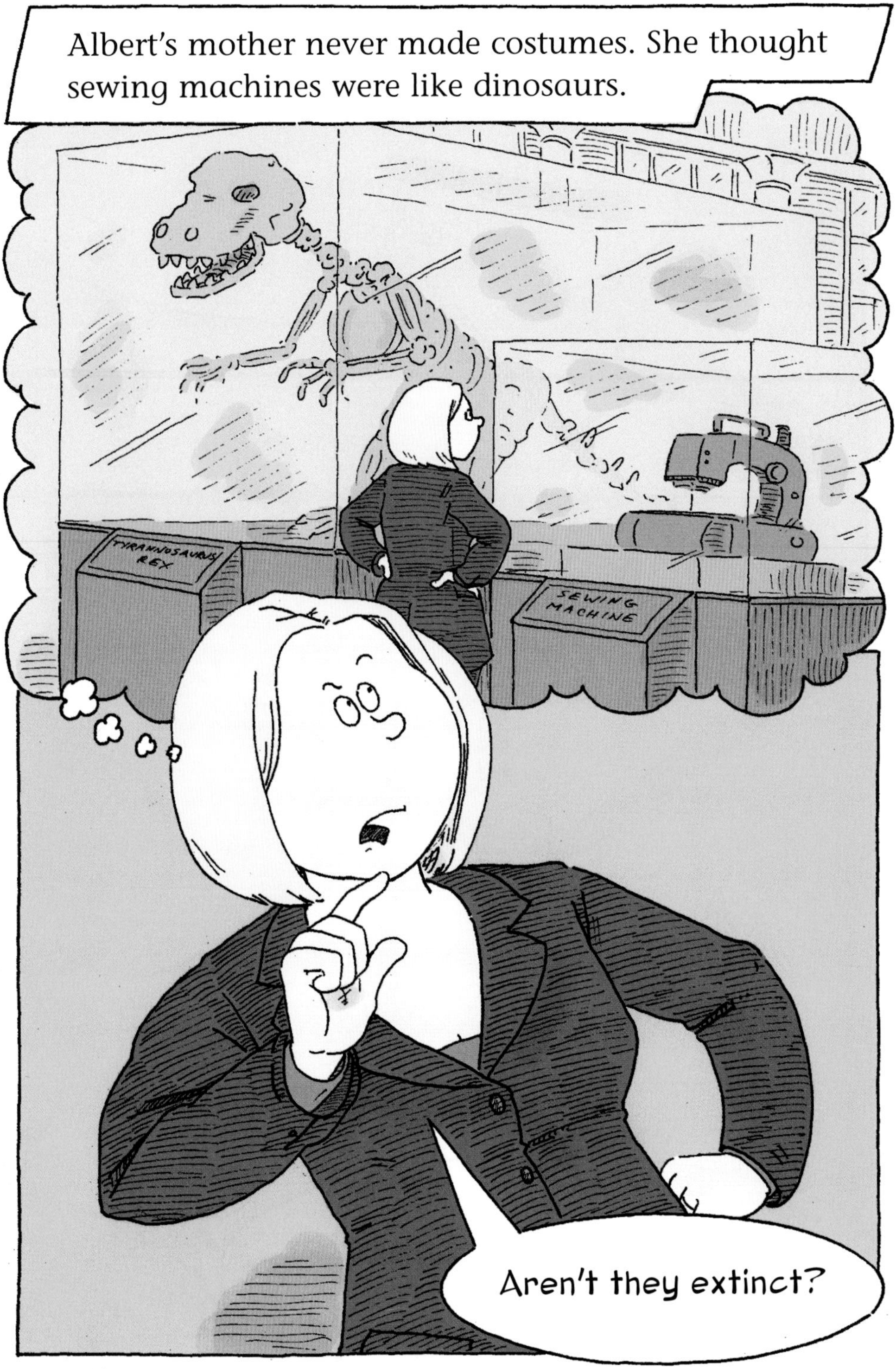
Albert's mother never made costumes. She thought sewing machines were like dinosaurs.
TYRANNOSAURUS REX
SEWING MACHINE
Aren't they extinct?

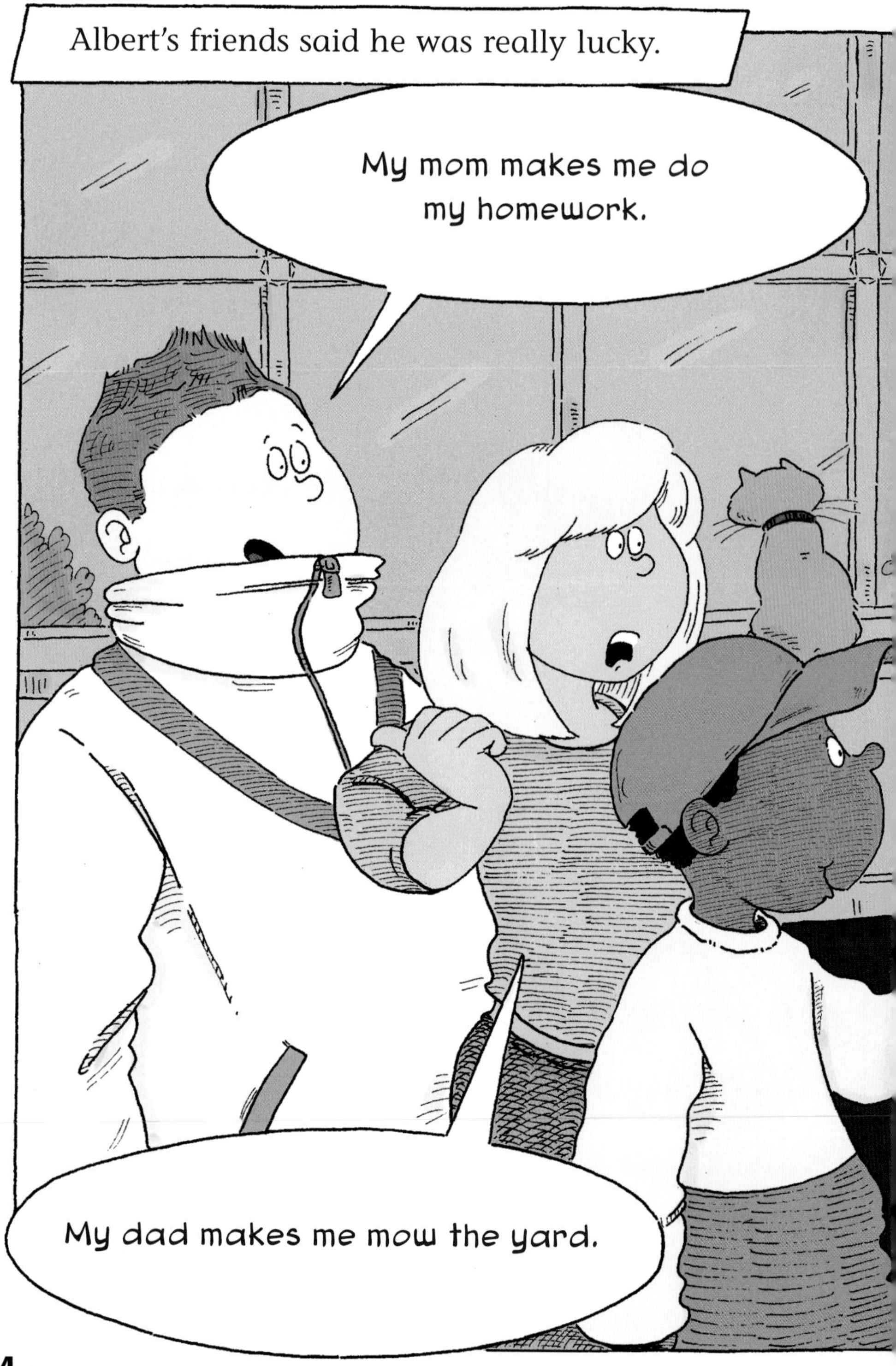
Albert's friends said he was really lucky.
My mom makes me do my homework.
My dad makes me mow the yard.

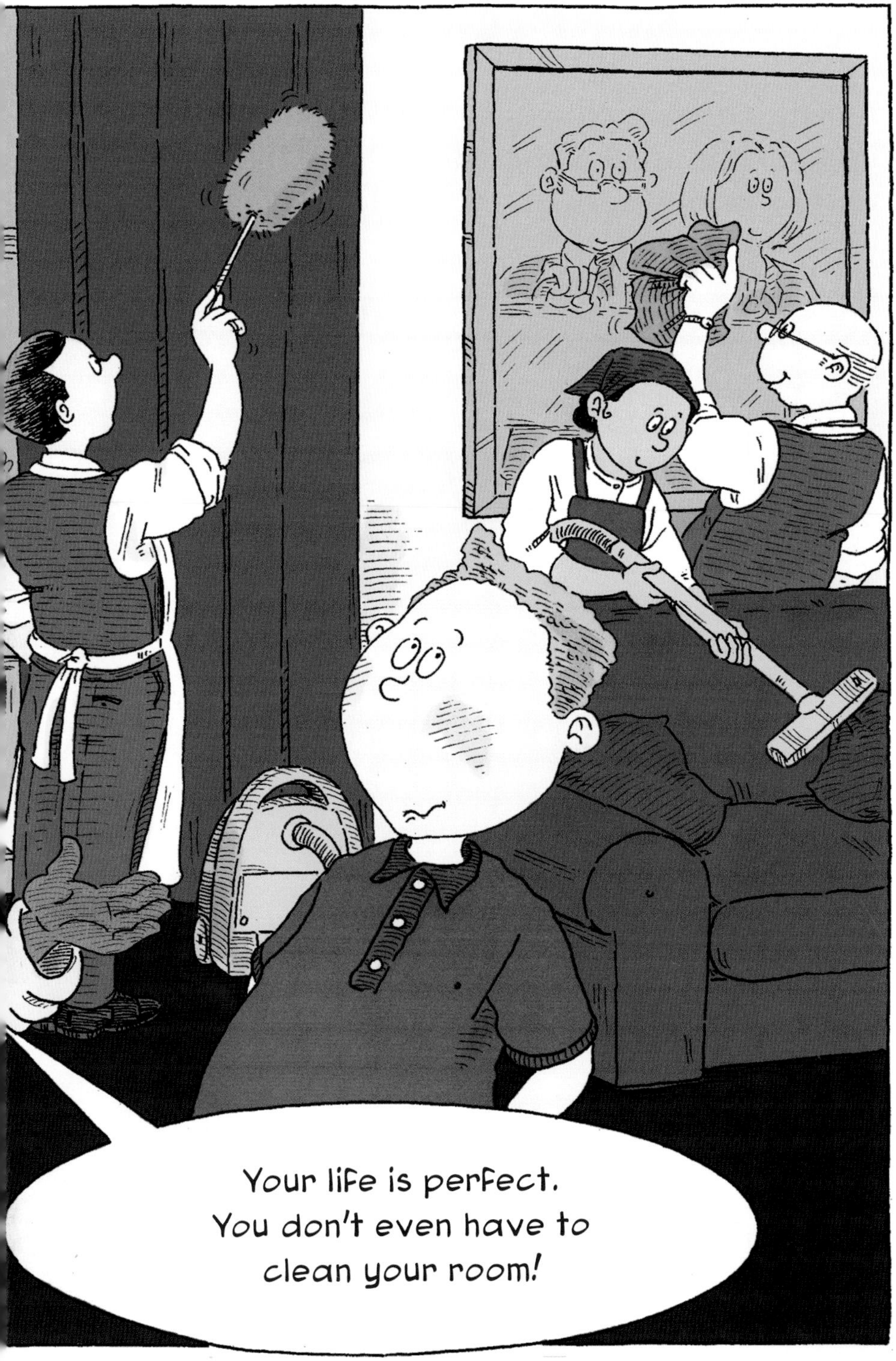
Your life is perfect.
You don't even have to
clean your room!

CHAPTER TWO

Albert's life was not perfect. There was one thing he wanted more than anything else in the whole world. Albert wanted his mom and dad to spend time with him.

No matter how well he did in school . . .

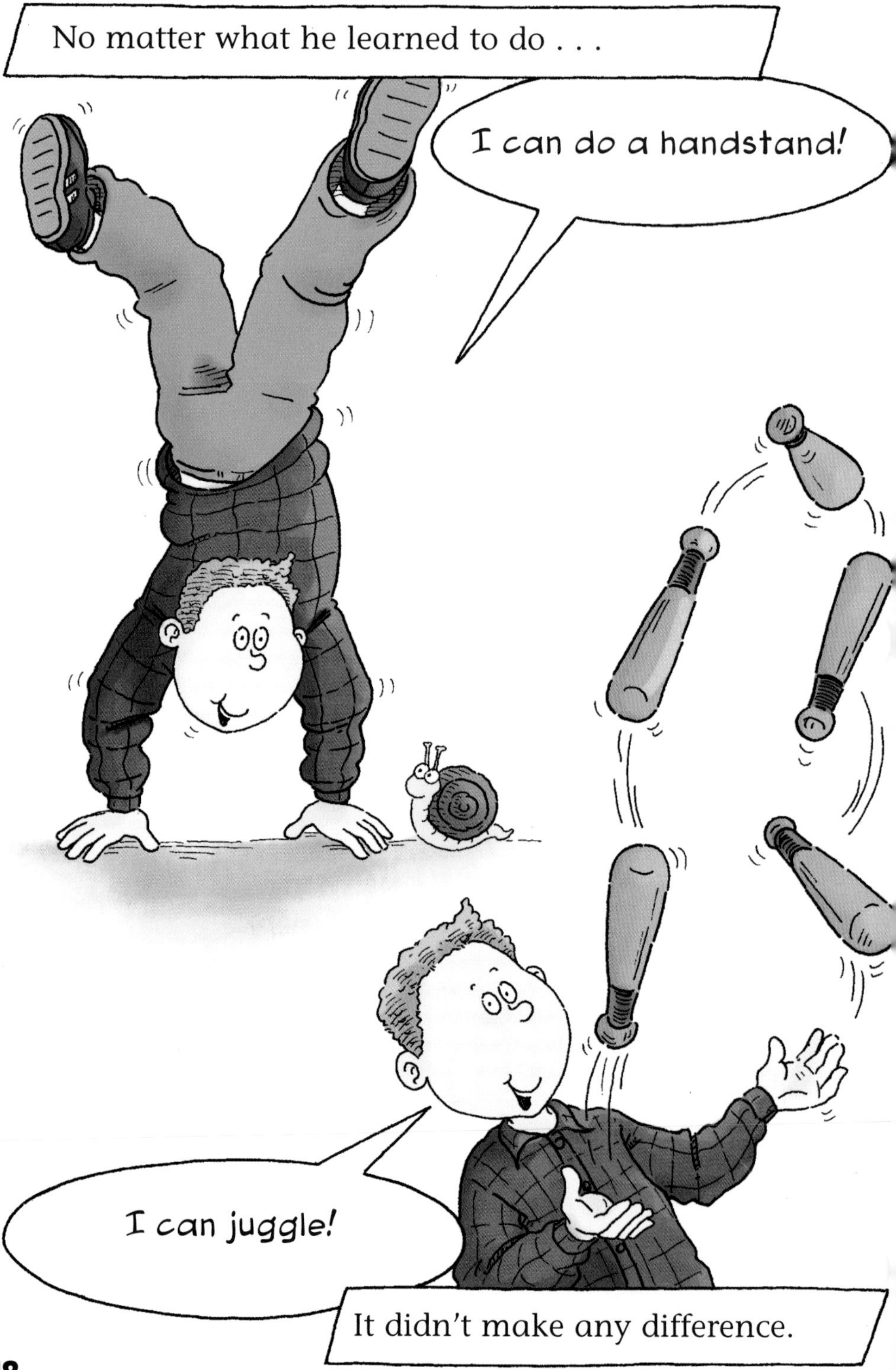
No matter what he learned to do . . .
I can do a handstand!
I can juggle!
It didn't make any difference.

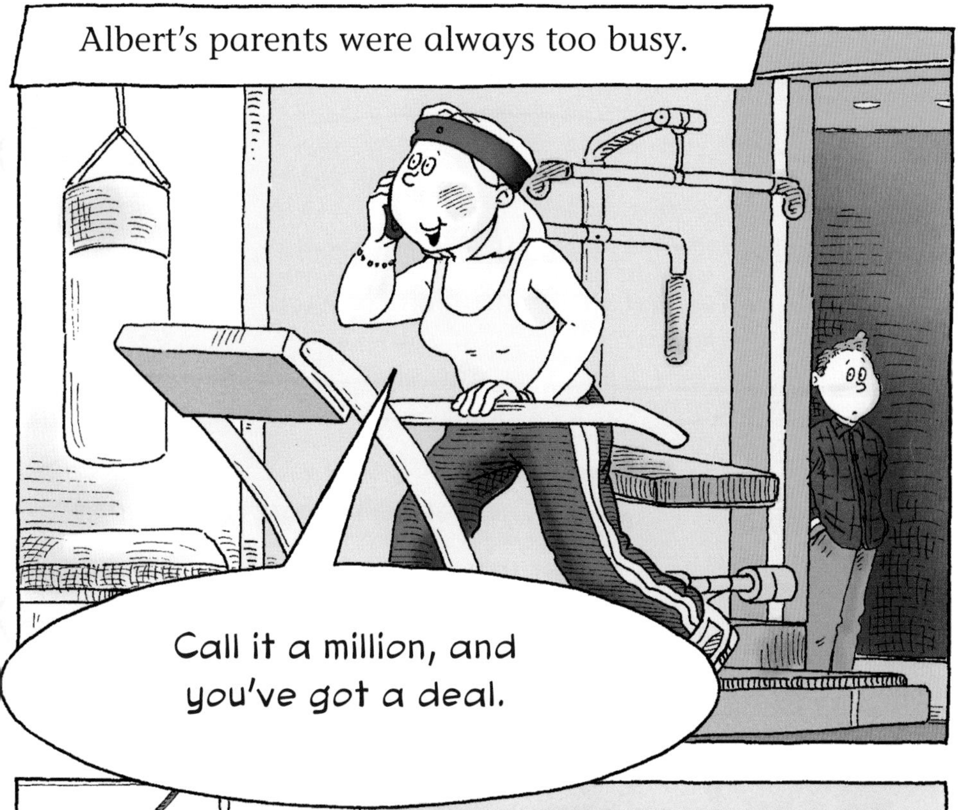
Albert's parents were always too busy.
Call it a million, and you've got a deal.

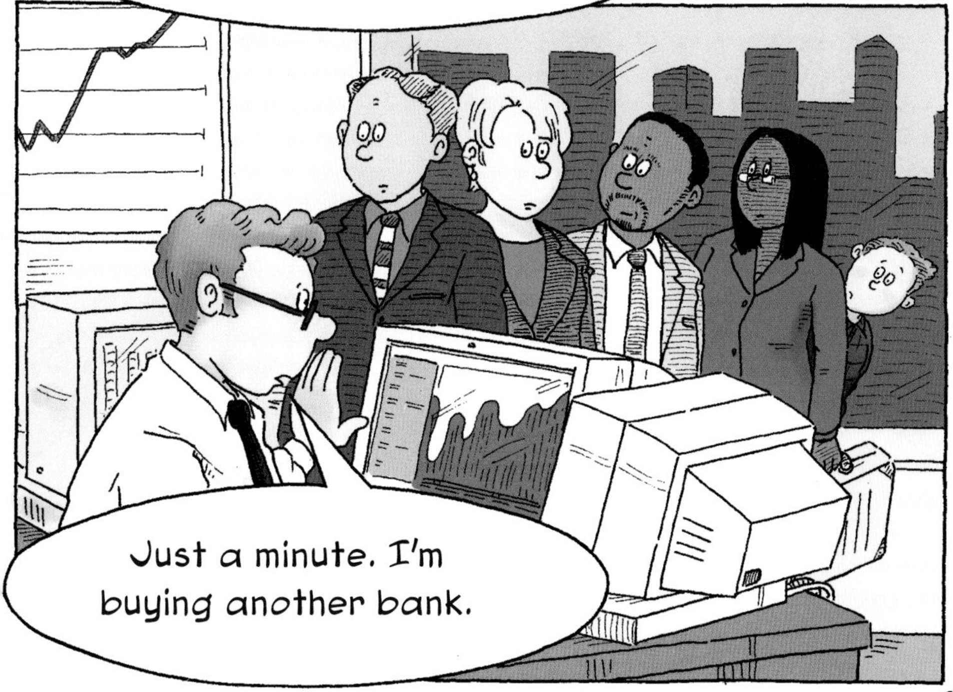
Just a minute. I'm buying another bank.

Poor Albert! He didn't know what to do. His friend, Dan, had a good idea.

That night, while his mom was swimming in the pool and his dad was lifting weights to keep fit . . .

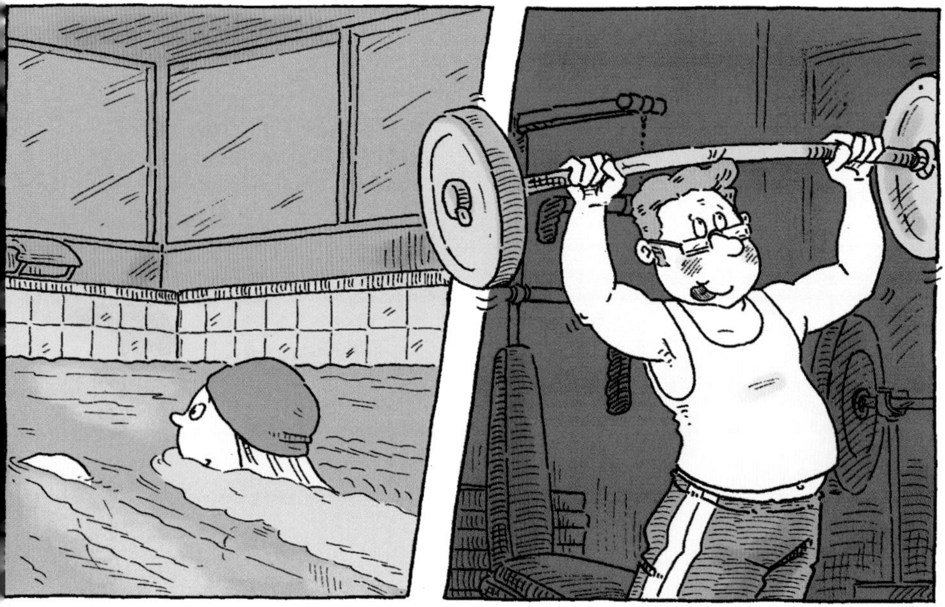

. . . Albert found his parents' calendars. He flipped over the pages until he found a Saturday that they were both free.

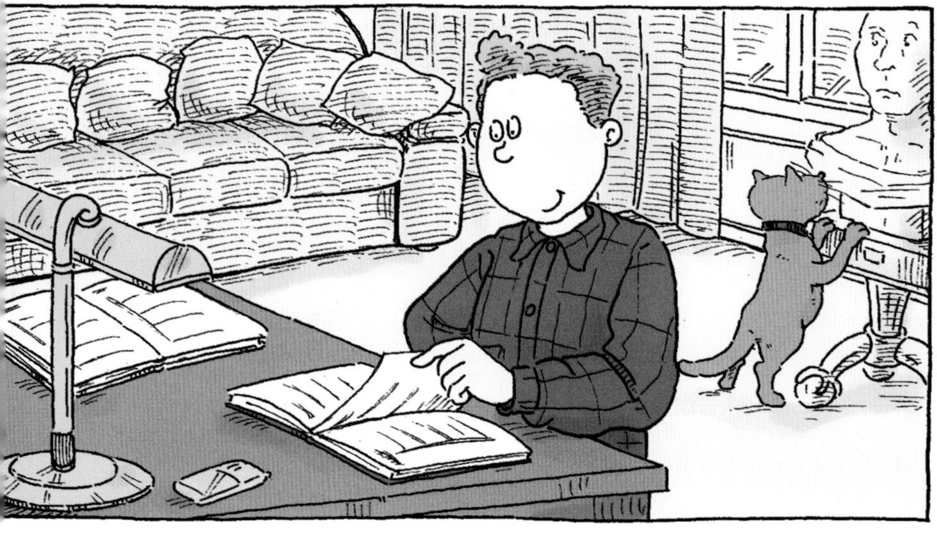

He picked up a thick red pencil, and he wrote,
"ALBERT ONLY" in big bold letters across the page.

That's that, thought Albert happily. Then he went
off to bed to watch TV.

Days passed, and Albert got more and more excited. There were so many things they could do on Saturday.

He could go to a football game with his mom and dad.

They could go shopping

They could all order pizza and watch a movie together.

Just to be sure, every morning, Albert asked the same question.

His parents always said the same thing.

Then they jumped into their limousine and went off to work.

CHAPTER THREE

Finally, the great day arrived. It was still dark when Albert woke up. He couldn't help himself. He was excited. It almost felt like Christmas.

But when he ran downstairs, his dad was in a suit.
His mom was talking on the phone.

There was a helicopter
waiting on the lawn.

Albert couldn't believe it.

What about our appointment?

His mom reached into her bag and gave Albert some money. Then his parents climbed into the helicopter and flew off to work.

Never mind, thought Albert, as bravely as he could. I'll play with my friends instead.

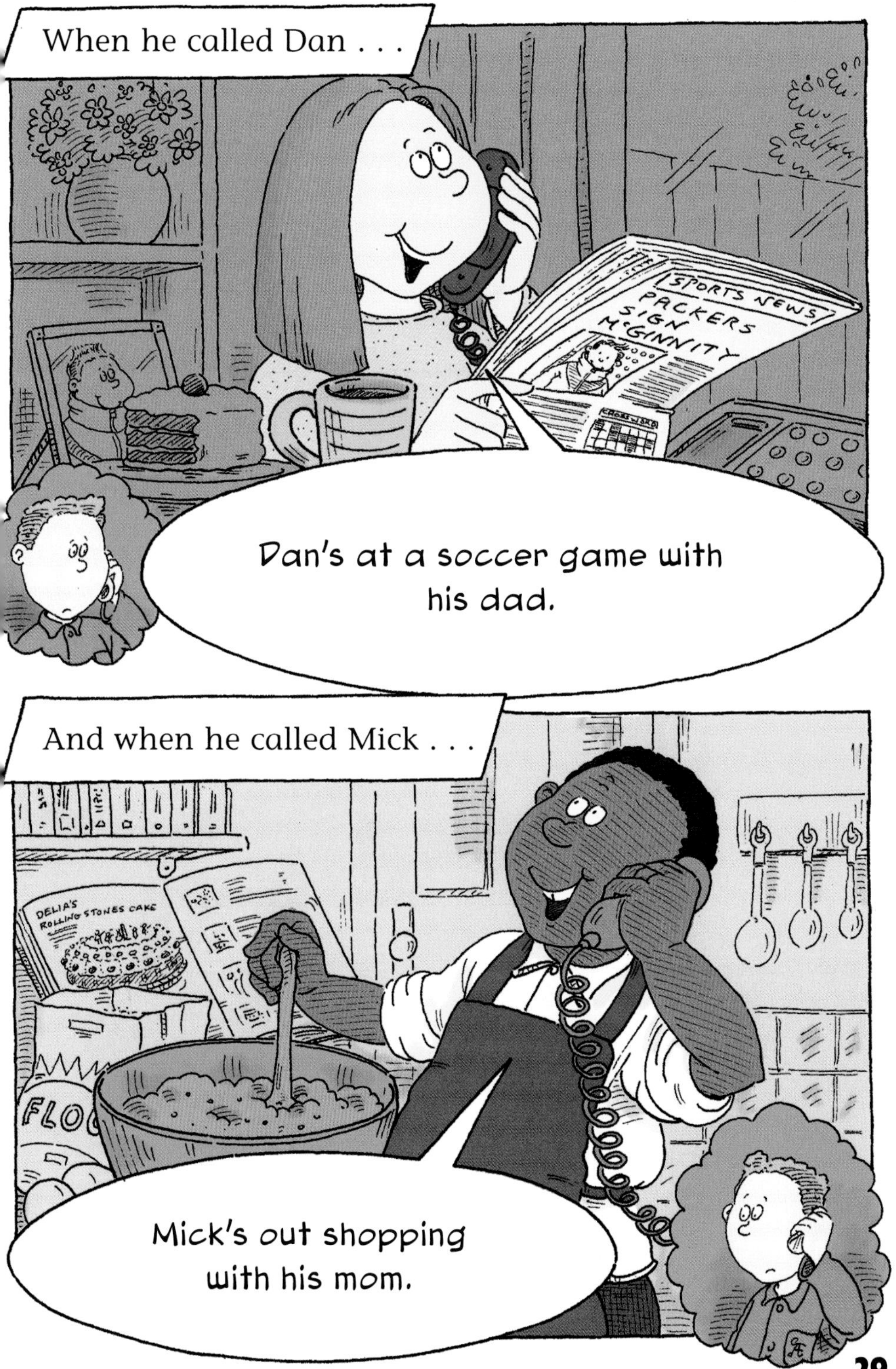
When he called Dan . . .
SPORTS NEWS
PACKERS SIGN McGINNITY
Dan's at a soccer game with his dad.
And when he called Mick . . .
DELIA'S ROLLING STONES CAKE
Mick's out shopping with his mom.

Never mind, thought Albert. So he played his favorite video game all day. It was about aliens and outer space.

He watched his favorite movie. It was about aliens and outer space.

He ate a pizza with lots of extra cheese.

Then he went to bed.

That night, something extraordinary happened.

Albert woke up and saw a strange creature sitting on the end of his bed.

It had green skin, yellow eyes, and TV antennas on the top of its head.

For a moment, Albert thought he was dreaming. The creature he was staring at looked just like the ones in his video game and just like the ones in his movie. It was an alien!

Albert was so excited he couldn't speak.

Also, he didn't know what to say.

What do you say to an alien?

33

But aliens can read minds. That's why they have TV antennas on top of their heads.

Its voice was a cross between a squeaky door and an electric toothbrush.

As the alien spoke, more and more aliens appeared.

Some came from under the bed.

Some came from behind the curtain.

Others were in his closet.

This Earthling's got more clothes than a movie star!

35

All the aliens sat on Albert's bed.

They stared at him with their glittering yellow eyes.

It was amazing!

Albert could read their minds.

Suddenly, Albert knew he would have lots and lots of fun with the aliens.

Albert ran into his parents' room. They were working on their laptops.

Albert's father took Albert back to bed.

They looked under the bed.

They looked behind the curtains.

They looked in the closet.

There were no aliens anywhere.

Now, isn't that strange?

Albert went back to bed.

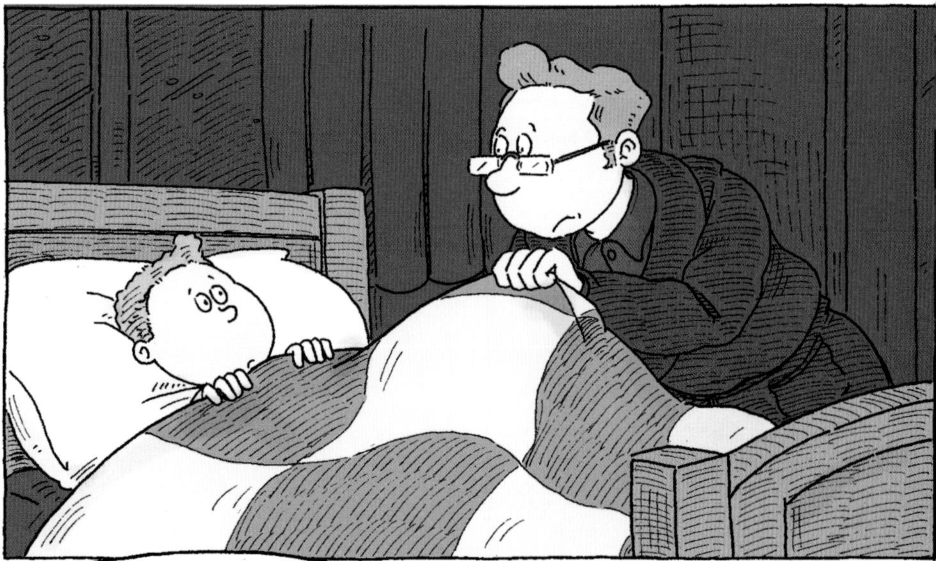

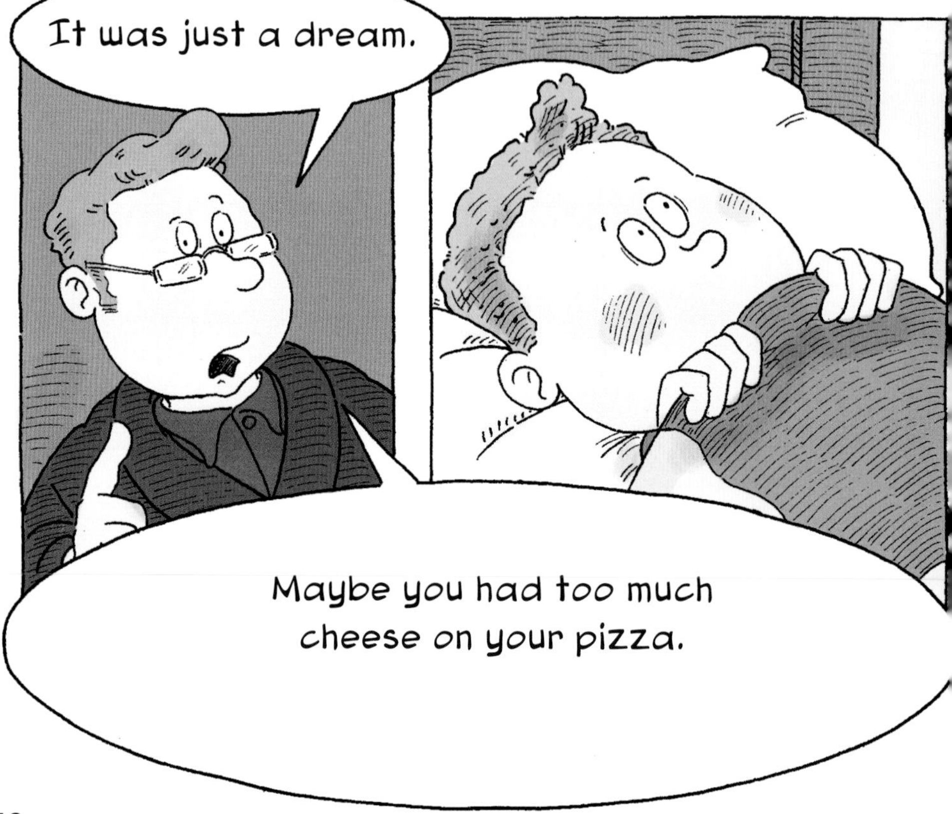
It was just a dream.
Maybe you had too much cheese on your pizza.

CHAPTER FOUR

The next morning, Mr. and Mrs. Twiddle were sitting in their limousine.

The limousine stopped outside a bookstore.

Albert's mother and father looked at several different kinds of books.

Albert's mother found one called . . .

That night Albert's mother read the first chapter of the book. It was called "Quality Time."

But quality time didn't mean an expensive watch. It meant spending time with Albert.

The book says that quality time will make him happy and successful.

More than anything else, Mr. and Mrs. Twiddle wanted Albert to be successful.

Albert's father made a big decision.

We'll take next Saturday off, and we'll spend it with Albert!

When Albert found out, he couldn't believe his ears.

It was the best news he'd heard in a long time.

But when Saturday morning came . . .

That night the aliens arrived.

This time they brought their spaceship!

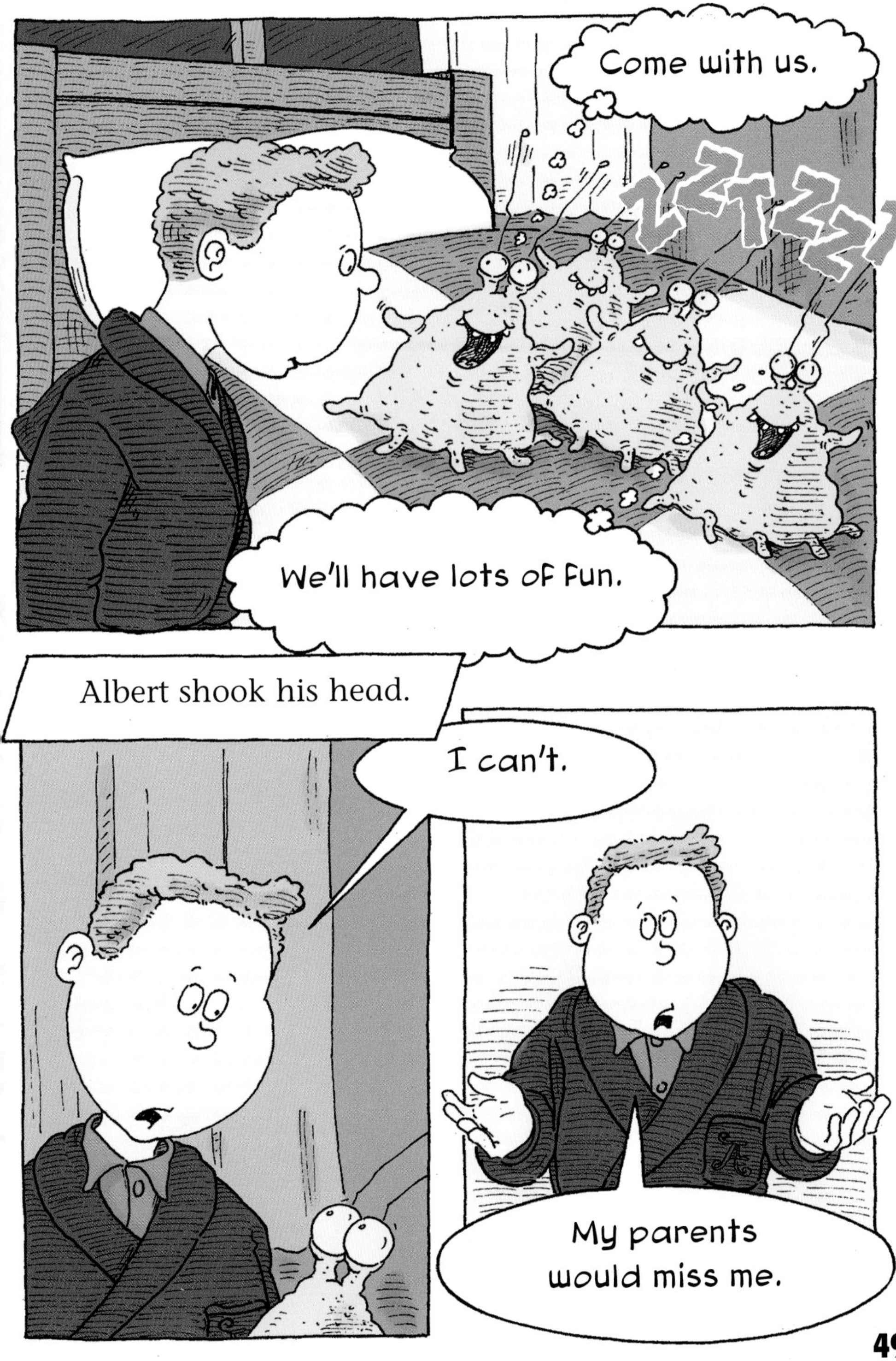
Come with us.
We'll have lots of fun.
Albert shook his head.
I can't.
My parents would miss me.

The aliens rolled their glittering yellow eyes and fell over laughing.

Albert ran to his parents' room. This time they had to believe him!

Albert's father looked angry.

The next Saturday, Albert went for a ride on his bike.

Everywhere he went, he saw families.

Some were riding in cars.

Some were playing in the park.

Some were shopping.

It seemed that everyone had a family except Albert.

When Albert came home, there was a note on the kitchen table.

So Albert did what he did every Saturday night. He ate a pizza with lots of cheese and watched a movie about aliens and outer space.

That night Albert had a terrible dream. He dreamed his mom and dad went to the longest meeting ever. By the time it was over, he had grown up!

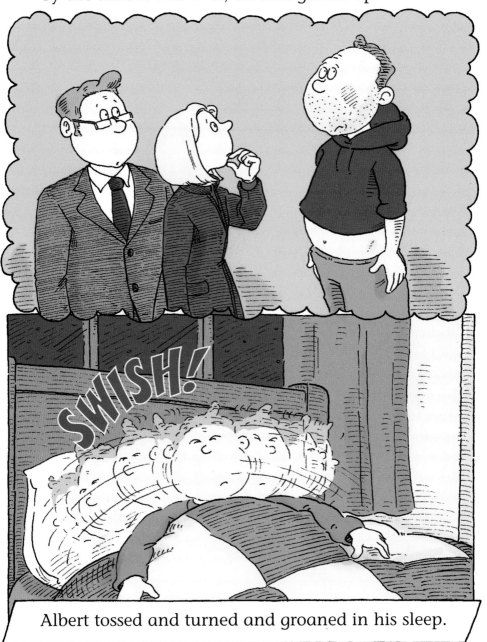

Albert tossed and turned and groaned in his sleep.

Suddenly, Albert woke up.

The aliens were sitting on the end of his bed. Their yellow eyes were glittering, and the TV antennas on top of their heads were going around and around.

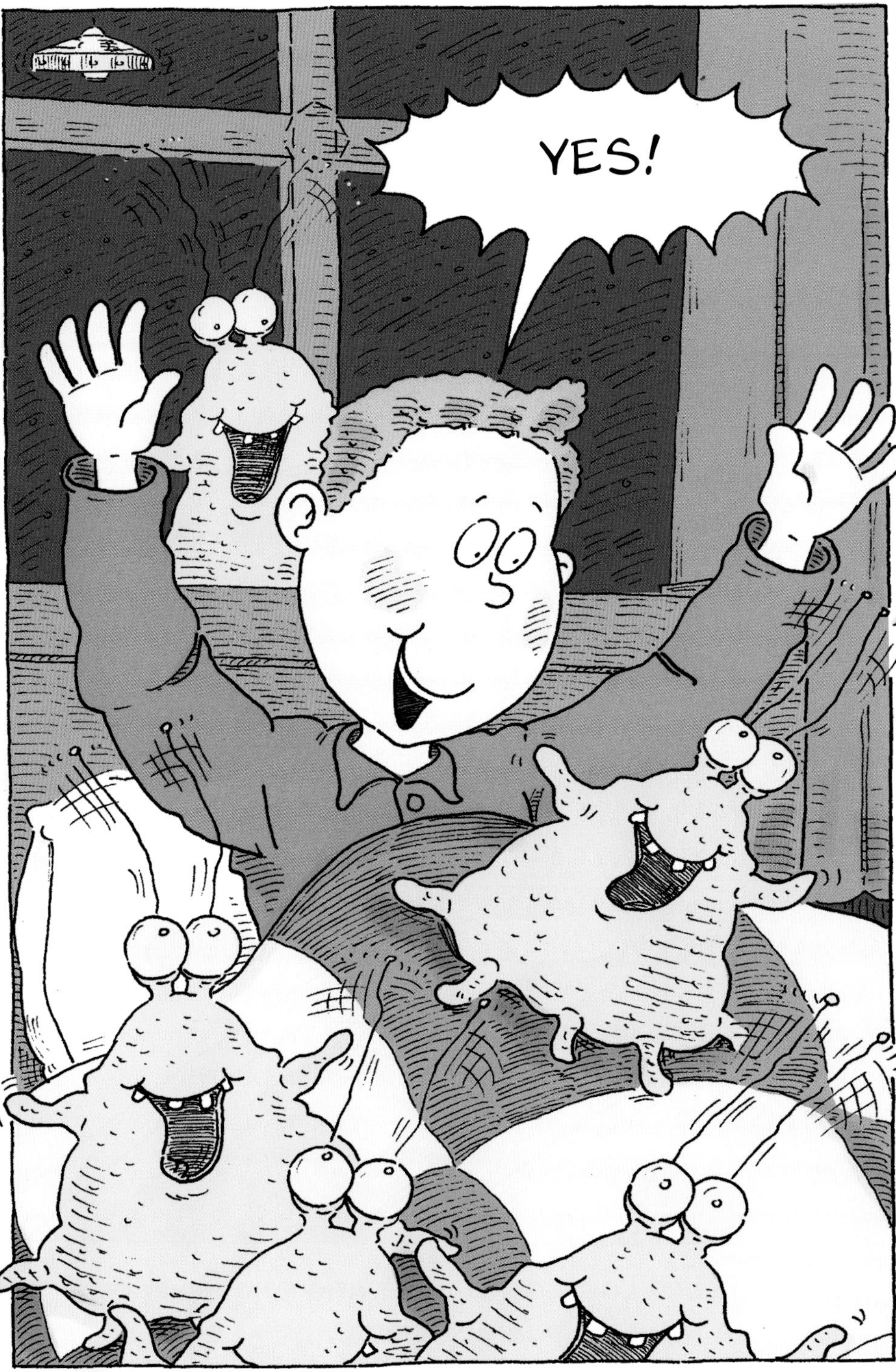
YES!

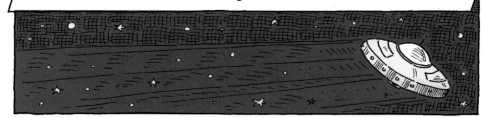

Albert Twiddle flew into space with the aliens.

As he watched Earth get smaller and smaller, Albert decided to write his parents a letter.

Then he sat in his special chair and pulled back
the throttle.

Mr. and Mrs. Twiddle were in bed when there was a knock on the door.

That'll be Albert.

I hope it's not more silly talk about aliens.

The door opened.

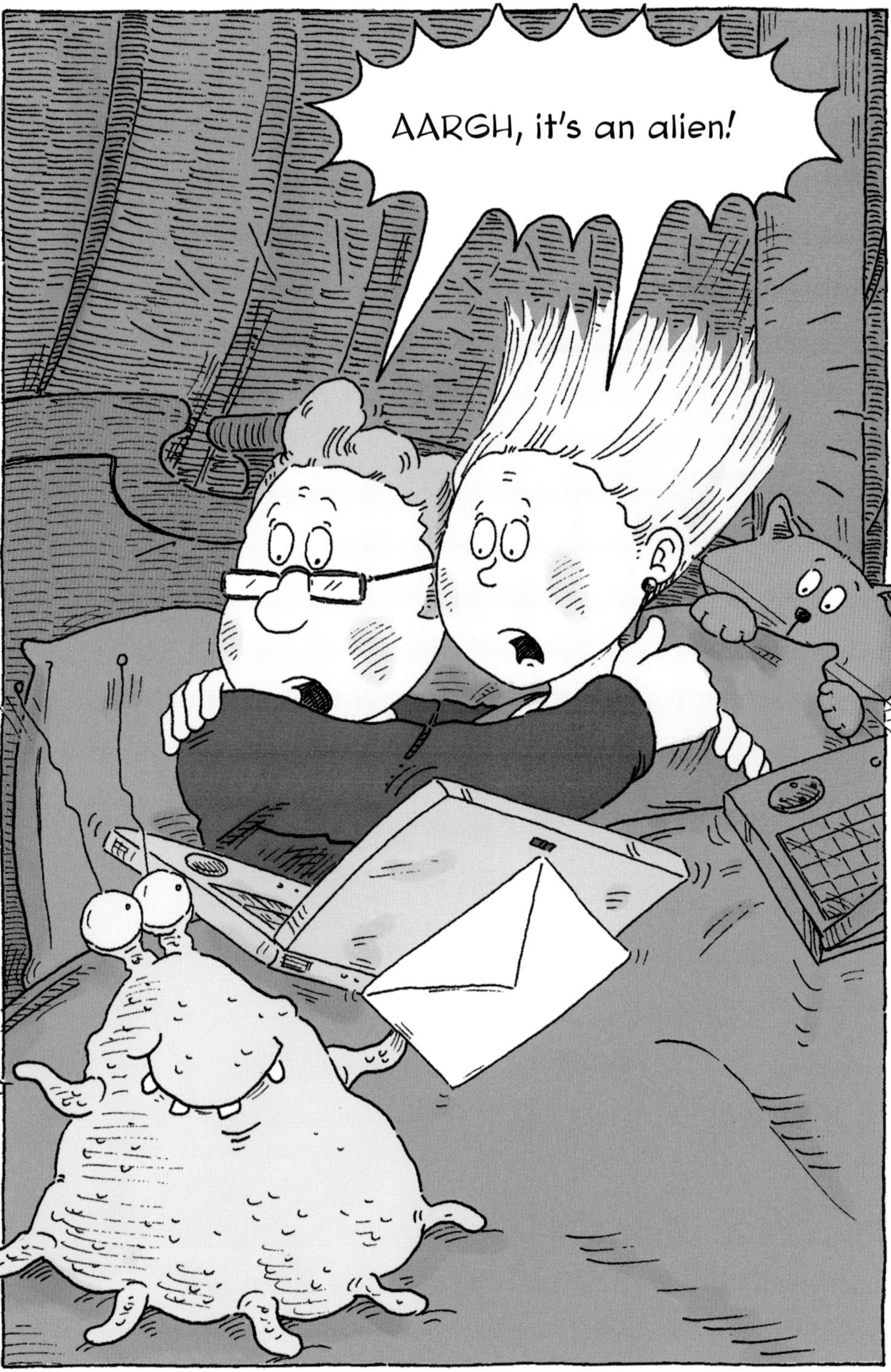
AARGH, it's an alien!

The alien looked at Albert's parents with its yellow glittering eyes.

The TV antennas on top of its head went around and around.

Albert's parents began to have the strangest thoughts.

Suddenly, Albert's mother began to cry.

Far away in space, the aliens turned their spaceship around.

It's time to go home.

Why?

You'll see.

The spaceship zoomed backwards, and somehow, it was Saturday morning again!

Albert ran into his parents' bedroom.

Mom! Dad! I'm home!

Mr. Twiddle was so pleased he gave Albert a big hug.
Mrs. Twiddle was so happy she gave Albert a huge kiss.

We have a surprise
for you.

First, they went to a football game.

Then they went shopping.

They also got a pizza and watched a movie!
It was the happiest day of Albert's life.
From that day on, Albert had a family like
everyone else.

ABOUT THE AUTHOR

Karen Wallace has written many books for children and young adults, including the award-winning *Think of an Eel*. She lives in Herefordshire, England.

GLOSSARY

antenna (an-TEN-uh)—a wire that receives radio and television signals

arcade (ar-KADE)—a place with coin-operated games for amusement, such as pinball games

chauffeur (SHOH-fur)—someone who drives a car for somebody else

expensive (ek-SPEN-siv)—costing a lot of money

extraordinary (ek-STROR-duh-nare-ee)—very unusual

extinct (ek-STINGKT)—an animal that is no longer existing or living

gadget (GAJ-it)—a small tool or machine

laptop (LAP-top)—a portable computer that is so small and light you can use it on your lap

limousine (LIM-uh-zeen)—a type of car, usually driven by a chauffeur and owned by someone wealthy

throttle (THROT-uhl)—a lever that controls a vehicle's speed

INTERNET SITES

Do you want to know more about subjects related to this book? Or are you interested in learning about other topics? Then check out FactHound, a fun, easy way to find Internet sites.

Our investigative staff has already sniffed out great sites for you!

Here's how to use FactHound:

1. Visit *www.facthound.com*

2. Select your grade level.

3. To learn more about subjects related to this book, type in the book's ISBN number: **1598890239**.

4. Click the **Fetch It** button.

FactHound will fetch the best Internet sites for you.

DISCUSSION QUESTIONS

1. If aliens really existed, do you think they would visit Earth? Why or why not?

2. When Albert tells his parents about the aliens in his room, they think he's crazy. Do you think people would believe you if you told them there were aliens in your bedroom?

3. People often say, "Money can't buy happiness." What do you think this means? Do you think Albert would agree or disagree?

4. Why do you think Albert's parents work so hard?

WRITING PROMPTS

1. Most kids would love to live in a big house with a pool and a roller coaster like Albert does. But Albert would give it all up if his parents would spend time with him. Write about what you would rather have — expensive toys or people who care about you.

2. Albert's parents want him to be successful. Write about why parents want their children to succeed.

3. Albert's mother thinks that "quality time" is an expensive watch. Write about how you spend quality time with family and friends.

ALSO PUBLISHED BY STONE ARCH BOOKS

Abracadabra
by Alex Gutteridge
1-59889-028-X

Tom is about to come face to face with Charlotte, Becca's double. Tom is confused because Charlotte died 350 years ago.

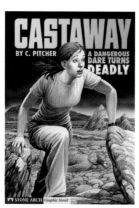

Castaway
by C. Pitcher
1-59889-029-8

Six kids on a geography trip are cut off by the sea. One of them is hurt, it's the middle of the night, and they have only themselves to blame.

STONE ARCH BOOKS,
151 Good Counsel Hill Drive, Mankato, MN 56001
1-800-421-7731
www.stonearchbooks.com